Oxford University Press

Oxford University Press, Walton Street, Oxford OX2 6DP

Oxford New York
Athens Auckland Bangkok Bombay
Calcutta Cape Town Dar es Salaam Delhi
Florence Hong Kong Istanbul Karachi
Kuala Lumpur Madras Madrid Melbourne
Mexico City Nairobi Paris Singapore
Taipei Tokyo Toronto

and associated companies in
Berlin Ibadan

Oxford is a trade mark of Oxford University Press

Illustrations © Val Biro 1984
Text © Jill Bennett 1984
Reprinted 1984, 1985, 1987, 1989
First published in paperback 1989
Reprinted 1989
This edition first published 1994
Reissued with new cover 1996

A CIP catalogue record for this book is available
from the British Library

ISBN 0 19 272305 7

Printed in Hong Kong

Once upon a time there was
a boy named Jack.
One morning he set out
to seek his fortune.

He hadn't gone far when
he met a cat.
'Where are you going, Jack?'
asked the cat.
'I'm going to seek my fortune.'
'May I go with you?'
'Yes,' said Jack,
'the more the merrier.'
So on they went, jiggetty-jog, jiggetty-jog.

They went a little further
and they met a dog.
'Where are you going, Jack?'
asked the dog.
'I'm going to seek my fortune.'
'May I go with you?'
'Yes,' said Jack,
'the more the merrier.'
So on they went, jiggetty-jog, jiggetty-jog.

They went a little further
and they met a goat.
'Where are you going, Jack?'
asked the goat.
'I'm going to seek my fortune.'
'May I go with you?'
'Yes,' said Jack,
'the more the merrier.'
So on they went, jiggetty-jog, jiggetty-jog.

They went a little further
and they met a bull.
'Where are you going, Jack?'
asked the bull.
'I'm going to seek my fortune.'
'May I go with you?'
'Yes,' said Jack,
'the more the merrier.'
So on they went, jiggetty-jog, jiggetty-jog.

They went a little further
and they met a rooster.
'Where are you going, Jack?'
asked the rooster.
'I'm going to seek my fortune.'
'May I go with you?'
'Yes,' said Jack,
'the more the merrier.'
So on they went, jiggetty-jog, jiggetty-jog.

They went on till it was almost dark.
Then they began to look for
somewhere to spend the night.

Soon they saw a house,
and Jack told the others to
keep still and quiet
while he went and
looked through the window.

He saw some robbers
counting their money.

So Jack went back and
told the others to wait till
he gave the word,
and then to make
as much noise as they could.

When they were ready
Jack gave the word.

The cat meowed.
The dog barked.
The goat bleated.
The bull bellowed.
The rooster crowed.

They made such a noise that
it frightened the robbers away.

Then they went inside the house.
Jack was afraid the robbers would
come back in the night.

So when it was bedtime he put
the cat in the rocking-chair,
the dog under the table,

the goat upstairs,
the bull in the cellar.
The rooster flew up on to the roof
and Jack went to bed.

In the middle of the night
the robbers sent one man
back to the house to
fetch their money.

He soon came back
in a terrible fright and
this is what he told them.

'I went into the house
and tried to sit in
the rocking-chair.
But there was
an old woman knitting
and she stuck her needles in me.'

That was the cat of course.

'I went to the table
to get the money,
but there was a shoemaker
under the table and
he stuck his scissors in me.'

That was the dog of course.

'I tried to go up the stairs,
but there was a man threshing
and he knocked me down
with his threshing-stick.'

That was the goat of course.

'I tried to go down to the cellar,
but there was a man down there
chopping wood
and he knocked me back up
with his axe.'

That was the bull of course.

'But the worst thing of all
was a little chap up on the roof
who kept on calling,
"Chuck him up to me-e!
Chuck him up to me-e!"'
And that, of course, was
the cock-a-doodle-doo.
Then all the robbers ran away
and Jack and his friends were rich.